To Ursula Barnett,
for her encouragement and wonderful friendship
—L. B.

For my mum—every brushstroke
—K. L.

About Sieta and Satara

Qolweni Township is just outside the holiday village
of Plettenberg Bay on the Western Cape of South Africa.
The people of the township care for the many children
who live there, just as Sieta is cared for in the story. Just up
the road from Qolweni Township is the Knysna Elephant Park.
A real baby elephant named Satara used to live there.

Published by Charlesbridge
85 Main Street
Watertown, MA 02472
(617) 926-0329
www.charlesbridge.com

Home Now was edited, designed, and produced by
Frances Lincoln Limited, 4 Torriano Mews,
Torriano Avenue, London NW5 2RZ

Library of Congress Cataloging-in-Publication Data is available upon request.

Illustrations done in watercolor and gouache on Bockingford textured
watercolor paper.
Display type and text type set in Blue Century and Usherwood
Color separations by Alliance Graphics, United Kingdom
Printed and bound by South China Printing Co Ltd
Production supervision by Laura Grandi
Designed by Vera Mueller

Printed in China
(hc) 10 9 8 7 6 5 4 3 2 1
(sc) 10 9 8 7 6 5 4 3 2 1

Home Now

Lesley Beake

Illustrated by Karin Littlewood

i◠i Charlesbridge

Sieta lay in her bed looking up at the black plastic roof of her new home.

"This isn't my real home," she thought. "My real home is over the mountains."

But this was home now. Everybody said so.

"This is your home now, Sieta," they said. "We'll look after you and keep you safe." She did feel safe. But it wasn't her real home.

Sieta stared into the black. There were pictures up there in the black, pictures she remembered from her other life over the mountains.

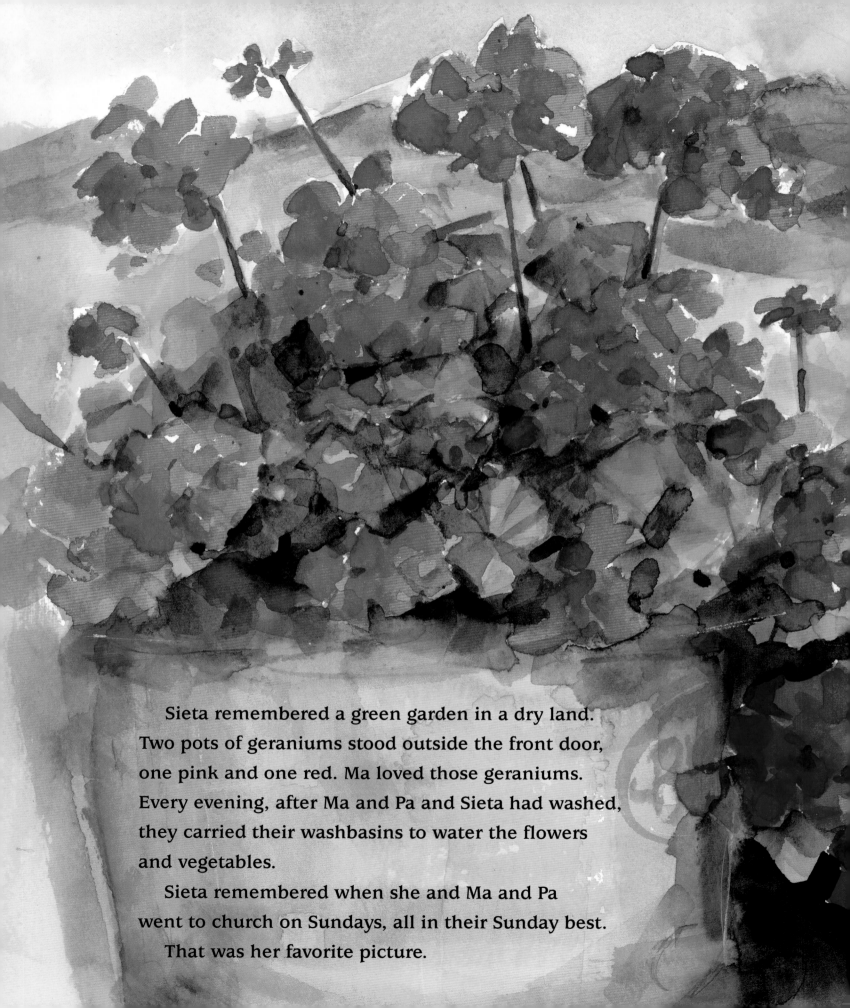

Sieta remembered a green garden in a dry land.
Two pots of geraniums stood outside the front door,
one pink and one red. Ma loved those geraniums.
Every evening, after Ma and Pa and Sieta had washed,
they carried their washbasins to water the flowers
and vegetables.

Sieta remembered when she and Ma and Pa
went to church on Sundays, all in their Sunday best.
That was her favorite picture.

But sometimes the other pictures came,
the sad ones. Then Sieta would shut her eyes,
squeezing them tight to try to stop the sadness.

Sieta saw her mother getting sicker . . .
and thinner . . . and quieter, and her father
getting gentler and softer and sadder.
One day they were just not there anymore.
Sieta saw women bringing her plates of food,
hugging her, and crying into her hair. She saw old people
coming with soft pink roses for her, and children hanging
around the gate and not knowing what to say.
Then she saw Aunty coming on the bus to bring Sieta
to Home Now—and now Sieta lived with Aunty.

Home Now was a busy place. People were building
new houses and new lives. Sieta watched them.

Home Now was a friendly place. People smiled
at Sieta. Sieta didn't smile back. She just looked
and looked at the pictures in her head.

Sieta went to school with the other children,
just down the dirt road from Home Now.
One day, Sieta's teacher took the children
to the elephant park.

"These are orphan elephants," said the lady
at the park. "They come from Kruger National Park.
They have lost their families and are staying here
with us, where they are safe."

"Just like me," thought Sieta. "This is their
Home Now."

"And this," said the lady, "is our smallest
elephant. His name is Satara."

Sieta held her breath. She stared
and stared at the baby elephant.

Satara was beautiful. His skin was gray
and wrinkled. It didn't quite fit him,
as if it were two sizes too big. His eyes were
small and wise.

The lady from the elephant park was
speaking to Sieta. Her voice seemed
to come from a long way away.

"Would you like to touch him?"
she asked.

Sieta took two steps forward. Slowly she reached out her hand and touched Satara. His skin was leathery and rough. Sieta smelled his elephant smell, and it smelled like wild places far, far away.

Slowly the baby elephant lifted his trunk.
He looked straight at Sieta. Sieta looked at him.
That night there was a new picture behind
Sieta's eyes—a picture of the baby elephant.

The next day, Sieta was still thinking about Satara.
After school, when the other children ran ahead
on the dirt road back to Home Now, she hung back.
Then her feet turned onto the road that led
to the elephants.

The lady at the elephant park didn't look
surprised to see Sieta.

"Have you come to see Satara?" she asked.
"I think he might be waiting for you."

Satara was by himself, eating some leaves. The big elephants had gone to walk in the forest with their trainer, but Satara was too small to go walking. He munched his leaves, picking them up carefully with his small trunk and stuffing them into his mouth. While he ate, he looked at Sieta, and she looked at him.

Sieta listened to the sounds of the munching baby elephant and the wind stirring the leaves in the trees.

Sieta's thoughts went far away. She saw a picture
in her mind of great, gray elephants walking through
the forest with one small elephant walking behind.
She saw Satara with his family in the faraway land
where he was born.

Then the soft sounds of the big elephants
coming home brought her back from her dream.

The next morning, Sieta watched the people of Home Now cutting wood, bringing water, making fires, cooking, and making things for their homes. They were looking after babies, children, and parents. They were looking after each other.

They were not always happy. Sometimes they were sad. Sometimes they were afraid. But they laughed and sang. They danced and played soccer. They were strong.

Then one of the children ran over and asked Sieta to play.

Afterward, Sieta walked back to Aunty's.
Aunty was putting two pots of geraniums
outside the front door, one pink and one red.
   "Hello, Aunty!" called Sieta.
Aunty held out her arms.
Sieta hugged her . . . and gave her a big smile.

A Note About the Story

Sieta's story is fictional, but her plight is a real one shared by many children in Africa. Millions are orphaned because their parents have died of Acquired Immune Deficiency Syndrome (AIDS).

AIDS is a disease that weakens the body's immune system. People suffering from it become ill with other diseases and die, especially if they are already weak from hunger. Medicines that slow down the effects of AIDS are expensive and hard to get, so AIDS is always worse for people who are poor—and many people in Africa are very, very poor.

So many people in Africa have died from AIDS that families and communities are sometimes unable to cope. Governments are overwhelmed by the size of the problem. Orphaned children are often cared for by grandparents or other family members—if there are any left. In some cases children have to look after other children, struggling with their own fears, unhappiness, and poverty.

Until a cure for AIDS is found, we need to find ways to prevent adults from becoming infected and to give treatment and care to everyone affected by the epidemic. AIDS is not going to go away. It is not something we can forget about. It is an enormous, growing problem for everyone—especially for the children of Africa who are most at risk.

For more information about the AIDS crisis in Africa, please visit the following websites:

UNAIDS: The Joint United Nations Programme on HIV/AIDS
http://www.unaids.org
Learn more about the UN's initiative to fight HIV and AIDS through prevention, treatment, and care.

Global AIDS Alliance
http://www.globalaidsalliance.org
Find out how the GAA educates the public about AIDS.

Hope for African Children Initiative
http://www.hopeforafricanchildren.org
Learn how this alliance provides support to orphans affected by the AIDS crisis in Africa.